LITTLE ONE - A CAT'S TALE

With love to

from
Edna

x

LITTLE ONE
A CAT'S TALE

Edna Dent

Matador
Unit E2 Airfield Business Park,
Harrison Road, Market Harborough,
Leicestershire. LE16 7UL
Tel: 0116 2792299
Email: books@troubador.co.uk
Web: www.troubador.co.uk/matador
Twitter: @matadorbooks

ISBN 978 1803131 993

British Library Cataloguing in Publication Data.
A catalogue record for this book is available from the British Library.

Printed and bound by CPI Group (UK) Ltd, Croydon, CR0 4YY
Typeset in 12pt Minion Pro by Troubador Publishing Ltd, Leicester, UK

Matador is an imprint of Troubador Publishing Ltd

Based on a true story

Beware the sly fox

ONE

The fox poked his long, pointed nose outside his den and sniffed the cool evening air. His cubs were beginning to stir and very soon they would be demanding something to eat. They were *always* hungry! It was a fine autumn night and a brilliant moon was lighting up the sky – it was a perfect night for hunting, he decided. Mr Daniels the farmer had some plump, tasty chickens in his henhouse, and if all else failed Mr Fox had spotted some sweet little unsuspecting kittens playing about happily in the farmyard while their mother was away. With any luck they might even be out in the moonlight by themselves at this very moment! He licked his lips, his eyes gleaming with delight at the thought of the delicious meal his cubs would be enjoying before very long. Streaking across the moonlit fields, he made his way to Woodlands Farm.

Everything was quiet at Woodlands. Glen the sheepdog was snoozing peacefully in his kennel. Mr and Mrs Daniels were snoring contentedly upstairs in the farmhouse. In the barn Topsy the grey and white farm cat was warning her kittens that it was past their bedtime.

'You are *not* playing out in the moonlight and that's final,' she said firmly. 'You never know what might be creeping about out there. Now settle down at once and go to sleep!'

The kittens knew from experience that there was no point in arguing when she spoke to them in that tone of voice, so without another word they snuggled down in their bed of sweet soft hay and closed their eyes obediently. All was calm and serene; the only sounds to be heard were the rustling of the fading autumn leaves and the occasional sleepy chirrup of a bird from time to time.

Suddenly this tranquil scene was shattered by a deafening uproar erupting from the henhouse! The hens were flapping about in a frenzy, squawking and cackling, feathers flying. Glen began to bark furiously, chasing madly round the farmyard in all directions. The lights were switched on in the farmhouse and Mr Daniels came running downstairs in his bare feet, carrying his shotgun. Meanwhile Mrs Daniels stood at the bedroom window shrieking at the top of her voice. Mr Daniels fired a shot and all that could be seen of Mr Fox was the white tip of his bushy tail as he fled from the farmyard, across the fields and out of sight with Glen snapping at his heels.

'Something will have to be done about that fox,' grumbled Mr Daniels as he stomped upstairs and climbed back into bed. Peace was restored at last, and everyone went back to sleep. Unfortunately for Mr Daniels, he was not able to do anything about that fox, because a few days later he was rushed off to hospital with appendicitis and poor Mrs Daniels was run off her feet trying to manage the farm on her own until he was better. The kind-hearted farmer had taken food and fresh warm milk for Topsy and her kittens each morning, but his wife was much too busy to think about farm cats. They would just have to fend for themselves!

What was poor Topsy to do? It would not be safe to leave her kittens alone while she went to find food for them. She had a feeling that the fox would soon be back when he discovered that the farmer was out of action. She was convinced that her family was in great danger. Five lively kittens were a handful and it was impossible to keep an eye on all of them at once. Sadly she came to the conclusion that the only solution was to separate her family. She decided to take each of her kittens to different houses in the neighbourhood where she hoped they would be taken in and cared for, and most importantly, where they would be safe.

One stormy night, the hungry fox was seen prowling about near the farm again. There was no time to lose! First of all Topsy made sure that her other four kittens were safely tucked up in bed, hidden away in the shadows from prying eyes. Then she picked up Little One, the smallest of her babies, in her mouth. Squeezing through a hole in the barn door, she dashed off into the darkness. She struggled through the wind and the rain, until she reached the nearest farm, where the Latimers lived. Mr and Mrs Latimer had five daughters. Topsy had often heard them laughing and chattering to each other as they helped out on their dad's farm or rode by on their horses, waving and calling out to Mr Daniels as they passed. She was certain that one of them would take pity on a tiny fluffy black and grey kitten left all alone.

Dripping wet and exhausted, she reached the deserted farmyard. Cautiously, she made her way towards the kitchen door. The light streaming from the window shone upon a small patch of grass growing against the wall. Glancing all about to make sure that there was no danger, the mother cat carefully laid her kitten down as near to the door as she could.

'It's such a dreadful night,' she thought anxiously. 'I hope it won't be too long before someone finds her.' Licking the kitten's face, she said quietly, 'Don't worry, dear. One of the girls will come along presently and take you inside. You'll be fine. I must get back to the others now. Goodbye, Little One.' Then she rushed away into the darkness feeling very worried and sad.

Little One as a cute kitten

TWO

The local farmers talked about the storm that autumn night for years to come.

'Worst storm we've had in living memory!' said Fred Wilson as he drank his pint at The Red Lion. 'Trees blown down, roofs blown off, fields flooded – WHAT A NIGHT THAT WAS!'

It certainly was a wild wet night! The wind tore relentlessly through the ragged trees. Grey clouds scudded across the cheerless sky, blotting out the dim light of the pallid moon. The icy rain lashed down, gushing down the drainpipes, splashing against the farmhouse wall and dripping onto poor Little One. She was freezing cold, soaked to the skin, hungry and trembling with fright… no one had come to help her. Topsy's plan had gone wrong! The unhappy kitten began to cry for her mother, for the cosy barn, for her bed of dry, sweet hay. She longed to be snuggled with her brothers and sisters in the warmth and comfort of her mother's soft fur. She was too weak and scared to move from the spot where her mother had told her to stay. Why had no one come for her? She mewed in desperation, but no one heard her.

Inside the farmhouse the Latimers were having a birthday party. The sounds of clattering crockery, chattering and laughter drifted through the open window. Someone began to play the piano and mouth-watering cooking smells wafted into the farmyard, but Little One was unaware of it all. As dark clouds swirled around her head and her large blue eyes grew dim, she gave one last pitiful cry before sinking back unconscious into the wet grass.

'Did you hear that noise, Stuart?' Anna asked as she closed the car door. Anna was the eldest of the Latimer girls. She and her husband had driven from the city to join the family for the party.

'It's difficult to hear anything in this wind and rain,' Stuart shouted. 'Let's go inside. We're getting drenched out here.' He ran to the kitchen door.

'I'm sure I heard a cry,' Anna insisted. 'It came from over here.' She darted towards the patch of grass. As Stuart opened the kitchen door, a stream of light shone out into the darkness and they saw the lifeless body of the black and grey kitten.

'Oh, look!' Anna cried out. 'It's a kitten. Poor little thing! Come on, Little One,' she murmured. 'Let's get you inside out of the rain.' Gently she picked up the bedraggled kitten and carried her into the house.

'My mother was right,' Little One thought in despair. 'Someone *has* come after all – but it's too late!'

Anna's sister Natalie brought a towel and a saucer of milk. After she had dried the kitten's wet fur, Anna held the milk to its mouth. The poor animal was too exhausted to lift her head and collapsed into the saucer. Mrs Latimer could see that the kitten was dying. It was hopeless to try to revive it, in her opinion.

'Anna,' she said sympathetically, 'I think it's too late to help the pathetic little thing now. Just leave it and put it outside.' But Anna was determined to try, anyway.

'No!' she replied firmly. 'It's still breathing and I'm sure it will recover if it's kept warm.' She wrapped her pink woollen scarf around the cold, damp little body and laid it gently in the hearth by the fire.

After the party, Stuart drove home while Anna cradled the pink bundle in her arms. The quivering kitten was unaware of the young couple and of the noise of the car as it sped along the dark country roads towards the bright lights of the city. She was lost in a strange and silent otherworld.

Suddenly, Anna spoke. 'Stuart,' she said, 'I've just had a thought. What if Sophie doesn't like having a strange kitten in her house?'

Stuart smiled. 'Don't worry, Anna, love,' he said. 'Everything will be fine.' Sophie was their pet cat. She was an elegant animal with long white silky fur, a fluffy tail and beautiful bright green eyes.

When they arrived home, Sophie dashed to the door

to greet them but stopped suddenly when she saw the little kitten.

'What is this kitten doing in my house? What is going to happen to me?' she thought. Feeling very anxious and miserable, she crept behind the sofa and stayed there for several hours.

Anna put the kitten in a little box near the radiator, but Little One was quite unconscious of it. She had no idea that Anna and Stuart stayed up all night with her, peering anxiously into the box from time to time and trying to feed her with little drops of milk from a syringe. Stuart held her while Anna squeezed the syringe into the kitten's passive little mouth. One or two drops trickled down her throat but there was no change in her condition. At first it seemed that Mrs Latimer had been right after all. Then at last, to their relief, at about three o'clock in the morning Little One became conscious. Finding her mouth full of milk she began to splutter and sneeze, spitting out milk everywhere.

Later that day, she was able to struggle out of the box and take a few wobbly steps across the floor. When Stuart came home from work the following evening he was pleased to see her playing with a scrap of paper for a little while before flopping down asleep. Anna and Stuart were delighted at her progress. They became so fond of her that they wanted to keep her. Their cat Sophie was not at all happy, however. She resented having a strange kitten in her house and she sulked behind the sofa until the visitor was safely tucked up in her box, fast asleep. When she woke up one morning Little One was surprised to find Sophie looking down at her.

'Good morning, Little One,' she said quietly. 'May I have a word with you?'

Little One purred as she clambered out of the box and patted Sophie playfully on the nose. Then, seeing Sophie's serious expression, she sat down obediently, looking at her intently with her big blue eyes.

'Now look here, Little One,' Sophie said softly, 'I'm very pleased that you've made such an excellent recovery. Anna and Stuart are really kind people,' she went on. 'Anna saved my life too, you know. I had cat flu and everyone thought there was no hope, but Anna didn't listen to them. She nursed me back to health and here I am as right as rain. But…' she narrowed her green eyes and spoke very slowly and deliberately, '*I'm* the pet in *this* house and *you're* only a guest. Now that you're better, it's time for you to move on!'

Having said what she had to say, Sophie tossed her head and stalked out of the room, her tail swishing angrily from side to side. The little kitten was shocked. She bowed her head and crept back into her box. Tears trickled down her nose as she buried her head in Anna's pink scarf and cried herself to sleep.

'What is to become of me now?' she sobbed.

Over the next few days, it became clear Sophie was not going to accept Little One into their family home. Sadly, Anna and Stuart realised that they would have to find another home for Little One.

The old windmill

THREE

Stuart's aunt was having lunch with her friend Isabella Gray. She told her the tale about the little kitten from the farm. Mrs Gray was intrigued. To her surprise she found herself thinking about the abandoned kitten when she returned home and she wondered whether she should offer to take it.

'That poor kitten. Perhaps I could take her in? Life in this flat can be lonely sometimes,' she said to herself.

Mrs Gray lived in a little upstairs flat near the sea. It was one of a small group of flats built in its own grounds near the coast road. The land had once been part of a farm which Mrs Gray could see in the distance when she looked out of her kitchen window. Just beyond the stone wall at the bottom of the garden was an old windmill standing at the top of a hill, its great white sails facing the sea. The old lady was quite content in her flat, but sometimes she felt that there was something missing.

She made herself a cup of tea and sat back in her pink, velvet chair, considering the advantages and disadvantages of having a cat for a pet. Now that her family had left home there were times when she felt quite lonely. A cat would be company. She would be able to talk to a cat. A cat would give her something to think about. Instead of returning to an empty flat, a cat would be there to welcome her when she came home. She would be able to stroke a cat as it sat on her knee in the evening.

On the other hand, cats were notorious for sharpening their claws on one's good furniture. One of her friends had to replace part of the stair carpet after her cat had made a hole in it with her claws. Cats were mischievous. Cats broke things. Cats were curious and went into places where they were not supposed to go. She looked round her immaculate flat, at the jade carpet and matching curtains, at her very expensive pink velvet chair, and wondered what she should do. She decided to telephone Stuart.

Stuart was pleased to hear from her. Two of the girls from work had been interested in having the kitten, but Mrs Gray's had been the only firm offer. He would bring the kitten along as soon as he and Anna were sure that she had fully recovered.

About a week later, Sophie watched Stuart carry the kitten into the car feeling content and satisfied that she was safe at last. When he reached Mrs Gray's flat, Stuart brought Little One up the stairs in a pet carrier, which he put down carefully on the sitting-room floor. He opened the door and out tumbled the sweetest little fluffy black and grey kitten. Mrs Gray fell in love with her at once.

'Isn't she adorable?' she cried, smiling with delight.

Little One ate some of the food that Stuart had put in her dish, drank some milk and then she climbed up onto the sofa. Mrs Gray picked her up and tickled her ears. The kitten snuggled under her chin, purring with contentment.

'She's made herself comfortable already.' Stuart laughed. 'She's going to be very happy here.'

Then off he went, leaving Little One with her new owner, perfectly happy. She had felt at home in Mrs Gray's flat as soon as Stuart had carried her upstairs. She liked Mrs Gray's smiling face and her soft, kind eyes. She knew instinctively that she was just right for her.

'Was this the reason why my mother left me at Latimer's farm that stormy night?' she thought. 'Had her sixth sense told her that her little kitten would come to live with this nice old lady in the end?'

Little One cuddling her toys

FOUR

Little One was so happy in her new home that she soon began to forget about her frightening ordeal on that wild autumn night, and fortunately she was none the worse for her dreadful experience. Mrs Gray and the little kitten settled into a pleasant daily routine. Every morning when the old lady opened the kitchen door, Little One came running to greet her and wound herself round her ankles, waiting to be picked up and cuddled. At first, to Mrs Gray's surprise, the kitten climbed up her back and sat on her shoulder while she waited to be fed.

'Little One must think she's a parrot!' her grandson Joshua remarked.

Visitors came to admire the new arrival and the little kitten had a wonderful time being the centre of attention. Friends who did not care for cats were charmed by her and took her on their knees to stroke her. Miss Stephen, the elderly lady from downstairs, remarked on her beauty and intelligence.

'It's no wonder the Ancient Egyptians worshipped cats,' she commented. 'They are so wise and superior.'

Little One was given lots of presents. She had a fluffy yellow ball, a bouncy red one, a rabbit bigger than herself and a green frog with a happy face. On the spare bed was a collection of cuddly toys – a big teddy bear, a floppy lion, a giraffe and a furry tiger. She liked to sleep in the middle of them. Sometimes she hid behind them, hoping to escape attention if Mrs Gray was calling her. Considering that a cardboard box with a crocheted blanket was quite unsuitable for such an exceptional cat, a neighbour presented her with a sheepskin bed and a fur cover. Mrs Gray bought a special toy on which her new pet was supposed to sharpen her claws. The old lady came to the conclusion that it was used to practise on, in order to be able to scratch the furniture more effectively!

The weeks passed by and in next to no time it was December. Little One sensed the buzz of excitement in the air. Soon it would be her first Christmas with Mrs Gray and her family. One morning just before Christmas, Mrs Gray and the kitten greeted each other as usual. Mrs Gray went across to the window to pull up the blind and Little One jumped up onto the windowsill to look at the outside world as she usually did. To her astonishment, the world had become all white and the air was full of tiny, white feathers floating down to the ground. She tried to catch some through the glass. It was snow, Mrs Gray told her. The rooftops, the gardens, the windmill and the branches of the trees were all covered with snow, which glistened in the morning sun. Mrs Gray said she thought it looked like Fairyland.

Not long afterwards, shouts and shrieks of laughter could be heard from beyond the wall at the bottom of the garden. Little One rushed to the window to find out what was happening. She could see children bobbing about on the hillside. Some of them were racing on sledges from the windmill to the bottom of the hill. Some were having great fun throwing snowballs. Others were making something bigger than themselves with the snow. It seemed to have a head and a body. Mrs Gray told her that it was a snowman. The children put a red, woolly hat on his head and a scarf around his neck. He looked amazing!

The following morning the kitten ran to the window to look at the outside world and the snow again. To her surprise most of the snow had disappeared, Fairyland had vanished and where the snowman had been, there was just a tiny heap of snow with a hat and a scarf on top. It was a mystery!

Mrs Gray arranged her Christmas cards artistically on the hearth. Little One found these very interesting and had great fun jumping onto the hearth and knocking them over onto the floor. She did this so many times that Mrs Gray decided it would be easier to put them all in a pile by the side of the fire!

Little One thought that the Christmas decorations were there just for her benefit. She found the Christmas tree particularly fascinating, the twinkling star lights especially. One day she chewed through the wire. Fortunately there was no harm done, but Mrs Gray had to buy new lights, of course. The kitten decided that the tree was really an adventure tree specially designed for kittens to play in. She slipped into the dining room whenever she found the door open to peep at the sparkling decorations and twinkling lights. She could not resist climbing up to have a closer look. It was fun reaching the top to see the fairy, magnificent in her silver crown and shimmering wings, gazing down with a superior look on her face. Mrs Gray had to fasten the tree to the wall with a piece of string to prevent it from toppling over. Thanks to the adventurous kitten it had fallen over twice already, much to the dismay of the bewildered fairy, whose face had a startled expression by this time and whose crown and wings were rather crumpled after her shocking experience!

One evening Mrs Gray decided to write some Christmas cards for her friends and family. She glanced at the kitten, who lay curled up fast asleep in the pink chair. Then she crept to the dining room, carefully closing the door behind her. For quite a while she was busy at the table, engrossed in what she was doing. Everything was quiet and still. Suddenly she was startled to hear a gentle tinkling sound. She was so surprised that she was convinced that something really extraordinary was about to happen. She recognised the sound. It was the chimes of the little gold angel on the Christmas tree.

She looked at the tree and, hardly daring to breathe, she waited for the mystery to be revealed.

All at once, the branches began to quiver and peeping out at her was a little furry face with big green eyes! Like a puff of smoke, Little One had stolen into the dining room unnoticed through a gap in the door which had not closed properly after all. As silent as a shadow she had waited until she thought it was safe to come out. It was not a mystery after all!

The family decided that the kitten's first Christmas was a great success. She had a wonderful time opening her stocking and investigating everyone's parcels. She scattered wrapping paper from one end of the room to the other; she dived in and out of the Christmas carriers and raced all around the flat, trailing the ribbons in her mouth. One of the children thought she looked like a Christmas parcel herself! At last everyone went home and the little flat was quiet and peaceful again. Mrs Gray made herself a nice cup of tea and then she and the kitten sat together in their chair and, half-asleep, thought about their perfect Christmas Day.

January arrived and with it came more wintry weather. At half past five one evening, Mrs Gray decided to close the sitting-room curtains. It was bitterly cold outside. The sky was dark and threatening. A harsh wind was gusting wildly round the building and flurries of hail clattered against the windows. Mrs Gray peered outside. In the deserted street below, she could see the solitary figure of a young woman struggling to hold on to a red umbrella as she was buffeted about by the icy wind. Glancing round her warm, comfortable room she felt very fortunate to be inside. Stretched out asleep in the pink chair was her black and grey kitten. Her glossy coat shone in the soft glow of the brass lamp standing behind her.

Mrs Gray walked towards the kitchen to make herself a pot of tea. As she passed the chair she leaned across and tickled her pet's ears.

'Well, Little One,' she said softly. 'Isn't it lovely to be safe indoors on a stormy night like this?' Opening her great green eyes, Little One gazed up at her, purring with contentment. She was a very lucky kitten indeed!

Little One at the washing machine

FIVE

Mrs Gray loved her pet dearly, but at first, she wondered if she had made the right decision. She was not used to having a little kitten running up her arms and legs, or jumping on her back and sitting on her shoulder, not to mention all the clicks in her good clothes! Once, on hearing tapping coming from the dining room, Little One went to investigate. Mrs Gray was sitting busy at her computer so Little One jumped onto the chair and then onto her shoulder to get a better view. Being an intelligent cat, she realised that Mrs Gray did not need her help!

Little One began to sharpen her claws on the new sofa. She scratched the furniture. She pulled the toilet paper from the holder and left it lying in shreds on the stairs. She climbed up the clothes-airer and knocked the clean clothes onto the floor. Mrs Gray spent a lot of time clearing up after her. There were also several accidents, which Mrs Gray called catastrophes.

'After all,' she said, 'they were caused by a cat!'

A Japanese bowl 'fell' into the fireplace. Broken china and potpourri were scattered all over the carpet. There was no sign of the culprit, of course. A vase of flowers was sent flying from the table. Mrs Gray found water and crushed flowers on the floor, but Little One had made herself scarce.

One day Mrs Gray was making butterfly cakes for her grandchildren's tea. As she was looking in the cupboard for the sugar, she heard a cracking sound behind her. When she turned to look, she found that the eggs had mysteriously rolled off the plate, where she had left them. Now they were swimming in a scrambled puddle on the kitchen floor. All that could be seen of Little One was a black and grey tail disappearing round the door without a sound.

Then there was the pink, velvet chair which was no longer Mrs Gray's pride and joy. In fact she did not think of it as *her* chair these days. There was no doubt who was the owner now. There it stood in the corner of the room with the brass lamp standing behind it, a shadow of its former self – tattered, torn and threadbare. Meanwhile in the corner of the kitchen stood a scratching pole specially designed for cats, looking like new! Mrs Gray had been right. It had only been used for practising on to develop her kitten's skills on the actual furniture. She complained to Mrs Paul, her cleaning lady, about the damage her pet was doing.

'I'm not sure if I can carry on like this,' she said in despair.

'Look here!' Mrs Paul told her firmly. 'You have to weigh up the advantages and disadvantages of having a pet. You have been a different person since that kitten came here.'

Mrs Gray had to agree. Her pet had changed her life and given her a great deal of happiness. She had become so fond of the little kitten, that she could not imagine life without her. All the catastrophes were forgiven and forgotten after a while. Nevertheless, the culprit recognised the wisdom of staying out of sight for a while. She had the impression that if she stayed at the scene for any length of time she risked being sucked up into the vacuum cleaner – on purpose!

Not long afterwards, however, there was another mishap. Mrs Gray was standing quietly at the kitchen sink, washing the dishes and looking out of the window at the birds in the garden. She was often amused by the gulls and lapwings as they paraded pompously about on the lawn. Suddenly in a flash they would fly frantically up to the rooftops and the sails of the windmill. The arrogant resident magpie had swooped down into the garden, disturbing them with his scolding cry. Evidently he thought the grounds were his private territory and he did not welcome company.

Without any warning the old lady was startled by a loud bang and felt splashes of water on her head and face. She could not imagine what had happened! Looking round, she saw that a large plastic bottle of sparkling mineral water had been knocked over. The bottle had exploded, sending the contents cascading all around the kitchen. Once again she had to clear up another of her kitten's messes! Once again Little One disappeared and this time stayed out of the way for the rest of the day. The water was dripping onto the floor, into the drawers and cupboards and onto the radio. Mrs Gray had to turn it upside down to let all the water run out. To her amazement it was still working after it had been dried with the hairdryer. It took her a long time to mop up all the water but at last everything was back to normal again. As usual, the kitten was forgiven when at last she crept out of her hiding place as soon as she thought it was safe to do so.

Little One playing in the sink

SIX

She redeemed herself by occasionally doing something that Mrs Gray considered to be rather clever. For example, there was the tap in the kitchen which was operated by a lever. It had to be pushed up to turn the water on and down to turn it off. As she was sitting quietly doing the crossword one day, Mrs Gray was surprised to hear the sound of running water coming from the kitchen. She went to have a look. Sure enough, the tap was running and the water was splashing into the sink. Luckily, there was no plug in the sink at the time! That intelligent cat had pushed the lever up and was sitting on the windowsill watching the water gurgling down the plughole.

Mrs Gray had learned the importance of investigating mysterious noises immediately, when Little One was about. A few days later, she went at once to the bathroom after hearing a clinking sound, to see what mischief her pet was up to this time. There she was sitting in the washbasin swinging the plug from side to side with her paw. As Mrs Gray watched, to her amazement, that remarkable kitten held the chain in her paw and dropped the plug into the plughole. Mrs Gray could hardly believe her eyes!

Apart from creating chaos, Little One enjoyed watching the washing machine. What she liked most was standing on her back legs with her paws on the washing machine door watching the clothes go round and round.

'She must be a very stupid cat to enjoy looking at washing going round and round,' remarked one of Mrs Gray's friends, who did not like cats. Mrs Gray did not agree, of course. As a matter of fact, neither do I. What do you think?!

Now, you may think that Mrs Gray imagined these incidents, but I assure you that they are absolutely true! Mrs Gray came to the conclusion that Little One had a particular affinity with water. As she became older she stopped drinking from her bowl and began to drink from the kitchen tap. Mrs Gray noticed that as she did so she constantly turned her head to look around as though she was on her guard. The old lady decided that this must be an instinct from long ago when cats lived in the wild; she wondered if Little One might be descended from the Scottish wildcat.

There was another incident which Mrs Gray found astonishing. Hanging on the wall in the dining room was a picture of a country scene with sheep in the foreground. One day Little One was discovered standing on her back legs with her front paws resting on a shelf, looking intently at the scene for some considerable time (long enough for Mrs Gray to find her camera and take a photograph). Mrs Gray could not help wondering if the picture had reminded the kitten of her life on the farm.

Summer arrived and the days were warm and bright. Little One enjoyed rolling on her back in the sunshine and playing in the garden. She had great fun chasing butterflies and darting in and out of the flowers and bushes. As she became more confident, she began to explore the grounds. By now she was no longer a tiny, fluffy kitten. She had grown into a sleek, independent cat. Her grey coat was smooth and glossy with distinctive symmetrical black markings. She had unusually large black ears, a bushy black and grey ringed tail, and each of her paws was black as night as if she had tiptoed through a tiny pool of ink or paint. Her eyes were large and green (not the blue all cats are born with), bright and mysterious as though she knew a thousand secrets. Mrs Gray was a little eccentric and inclined to be rather melodramatic at times.

'It's obvious that she's an exceptional cat!' she said. 'After all, she was rescued from the very jaws of death when she was a tiny kitten.'

One day Little One wandered off in the garden and did not return for the rest of the day. Mrs Gray was worried, but she was very tired and needed to go to bed. It was a warm night and she was quite sure that Little One would be safe in the garden. But Little One was not as safe as she thought. While she was exploring, she had noticed that one of the garage doors had been left open and she slipped inside. To her horror, she heard the door close behind her. She cried and cried but nobody heard her. Realising that no one was coming, she decided she might as well go to sleep. Looking around, she found a duster lying on the floor and thought that would have to make do for a bed. No soft cushion, no comfy basket, no supper, no treat. She felt so alone and unhappy, but at last, she fell fast asleep.

The following morning, to her relief, she heard the sound of the door being unlocked. As the door opened, the garage was filled with a stream of light. She dashed towards it and ran off down the path to Mrs Gray's flat. Mrs Gray was delighted to find Little One sitting on the doorstep when she went downstairs to collect the milk. Mrs Gray noticed that one of Little One's paws was caught in her collar. Carefully, she undid the collar and freed her paw. Fortunately no damage had been done. That clever cat had come home on three legs.

Little One playing hide and seek

SEVEN

Little One and the old lady lived happily together in the little flat for quite some time until Mrs Gray began to notice a change in her pet's behaviour. When she was small, Little One was delighted when visitors came to the flat. She enjoyed playing with them and she loved being the centre of attention. She purred happily when Mrs Gray's grandchildren petted her and made a fuss of her. But now as soon as she heard the doorbell, she rushed away into the bedroom and hid behind the bed or under the duvet.

Sometimes she would leap up to the top of the cupboard in the kitchen and did not reappear until the visitors had left. She rarely sat on Mrs Gray's knee these days unless Mrs Gray happened to be doing the crossword. Then that contrary cat would be determined to plonk herself down right in the middle of the newspaper and refuse to budge. When Mrs Gray picked her up she struggled and squirmed and bit and scratched in a fury!

If Mrs Gray spoke to her, she would stare back at her with a strange look in her great green eyes, or she would ignore her entirely and begin to wash behind her ears. Sometimes she would toss her head and stalk out of the room with her tail in the air as if she had been deeply offended.

At other times she would arch her back and glare at the old lady with a wild look in her eyes, her tail swishing angrily from side to side. Mrs Gray began to wonder if perhaps she should call her Wild One instead of Little One. At first she was puzzled by the change in her pet's behaviour. Then she reminded herself that she was a farm cat; not a domesticated cat. Now that she was no longer a helpless kitten, she was probably finding life rather boring in the little flat. Perhaps she was longing for freedom, for excitement and adventure.

Mrs Gray remembered the story that she had read when she was a little girl, about the cat that walked by himself. The story told how long ago the animals were taught to serve Man. The cat was never completely tamed. There were times when he wanted to be free. '*When the moon gets up and night comes, he is the cat that walks by himself, and all places are alike to him. Then he goes out to the Wet, Wild Woods, or up on the Wet, Wild Trees, or on the Wet, Wild Roofs, waving his tail and walking wild alone.*'

'Perhaps Little One was like the cat that walked by himself,' she thought.

Little One realised that she was changing too. She was fond of the old lady, but she was finding life in the tiny flat very dull. She felt restless and trapped. She wanted to run like the wind in the gardens. She longed to be able to climb the trees. She wondered what it was like on the hill beyond the garden wall. She would like to visit the farm along the road. She was too scared to go off on her own at present, but she made up her mind that eventually she would set off on an adventure when the time was right. In the meantime she would start training.

She practised tearing up and down the stairs like a tornado. She whizzed round the flat like a whirlwind. She scrambled up and down the clothes-airer in seconds, not forgetting to knock the clean clothes onto the floor as she went, of course. Whenever the opportunity arose, she took flying leaps everywhere in preparation for her great adventure. They did not always go according to plan at first.

One day she jumped down from the top of the kitchen cupboard. She knocked over the bottle of milk standing on the bench. It fell to the floor with a crash. Mrs Gray was very upset when she found the broken glass and the milk splattered about on the floor – another mess to clean up! On another occasion she took a flying leap from the chest of drawers in the bedroom. She had intended to land on the bed, but unfortunately she landed on the back of Mrs Gray's neck as she was bending down making the bed. As cats do, she used her claws to steady herself. Mrs Gray was shaken, to say the least, but she realised that it was a mistake and once again the acrobat was forgiven. Then she jumped from the side of the bath into the washbasin. She did not realise that it had been filled with water. As you can imagine – her flying leap this time was quite amazing. Fortunately her technique began to improve, to Mrs Gray's relief. It was then that she made her most spectacular leap.

One Sunday morning Mrs Gray had a very long telephone conversation with an old friend of hers. Little One was fast asleep under the duvet in the bedroom at the time. After putting the telephone down, Mrs Gray went into the kitchen to give her pet her dinner. Usually Little One came running as soon as she heard the clink of her dish. This time she did not appear. Mrs Gray thought this was most unusual and she looked all around the flat for her – in the wardrobes, behind the beds, under the duvet, on top of the kitchen cupboards. She was nowhere to be seen. When Mrs Gray looked in the dining room she noticed that the window had been left open.

There was only one explanation – the adventurous cat must have jumped out of the window into the garden below. Perhaps she was hurt and unable to move; she might have broken her leg! Anxiously, Mrs Gray hurried downstairs and looked all around the grounds, but there was no sign of her pet. She called her name again and again but Little One did not come. Feeling very concerned and upset, Mrs Gray made her way back to her front door. Before going in, she took one last look under the hydrangea bush in the corner of the front garden. There was Little One curled up asleep, none the worse for her experience. Seeing the old lady, she stretched and yawned, then, ignoring her completely, casually strolled into the flat waving her tail in the air, quite unconcerned.

One evening shortly after this, Mrs Gray had guests. As usual Little One had disappeared into the bedroom. She was sitting on the windowsill watching the world outside. The moon was like a giant silver ball suspended in the dark velvet sky. She thought the world outside looked mysterious and inviting. She felt excited and confident. Now it was time to set out on her adventure! As the visitors were leaving just before midnight, she slipped out of the door and ran off into the garden. Mrs Gray went downstairs several times and called her, but there was no response. At last she locked the door and went upstairs to bed. She was tired and rather sad. Perhaps the little farm cat had decided that she wanted to go back to her old life. Mrs Gray had always respected her wildness and independence. She would just have to wait and see.

Little One meets Oscar

EIGHT

Little One had heard her calling, but she paid no attention. She paused for a moment and looked round at the garden. It had been transformed by the moonlight into a fantastic land of mystery and magic. There were silver trees with delicate silver leaves. The grass, the flowers and the bushes seemed to gleam with a soft, silvery light. Everything looked mystical and fascinating. Taking a deep breath, she flew round the grounds like the wind. She chased the silvery leaves that had fluttered down onto the grass. She climbed up and down the trees and swayed precariously on the moonlit branches. She felt as free as a bird. This was fun! Suddenly, to her astonishment she heard a deep voice coming from the branch above.

'Excuse me,' the voice said irritably, 'I'm trying to hunt for my family's breakfast and you're frightening all the mice away.'

Little One was so startled that she almost lost her balance. Steadying herself with her claws, she glanced up and saw two enormous eyes staring down at her. They belonged to a large, handsome bird with speckled brown and grey feathers.

'I'm very sorry,' she replied. 'You were so silent and still, I didn't realise that there was anyone there. Who are you? I've never seen you before.'

'My name is Oscar,' the bird answered. 'I'm a tawny owl. We owls are nocturnal birds. We usually sleep during the day and come out at night. That's why you haven't seen me about.'

'I thought it seemed odd to be having breakfast at this time of night,' Little One replied.

'I have a remarkable party trick,' said the owl proudly. 'I am able to turn my head 270 degrees in either direction. Would you like a demonstration?'

'Yes please,' said Little One, and she was absolutely amazed at what he was able to do.

'Can you see that clump of trees over there near the farm?' Oscar asked. 'That's where my nest is. My owlets are hungry as usual and they're waiting for something to eat. I must be going. I'll find somewhere else to hunt. You seem to be enjoying yourself so much, I don't want to spoil your fun.' Just as he was about to leave, he turned and spoke again.

'Do forgive me,' he added, 'I haven't asked about you. What is your name and what are you doing out here alone at this time of night?'

Little One told him all about herself and about her adventure.

'Well, I must warn you,' he said seriously, 'adventures may sound exciting, but they can also be risky. There's a fox's den not far away and he often comes here on the lookout for rabbits to take home for his cubs to eat. He's a vicious creature and sometimes he kills just for fun. He stalks his prey very cleverly and then, when they least expect it, he pounces and there's no escape. Be very careful, my dear.'

As he was talking, Little One noticed a cloud of tiny dark creatures flitting amongst the trees at the bottom of the garden.

'I thought birds went to sleep at night,' she said.

'They are not birds,' the owl replied. 'They are bats. Bats look rather like mice with wings. They only come out after dark and they all disappear during the day.'

Little One wondered where they all went to.

'By the way,' he said, 'you are welcome to come and visit us at the farm. I'm sure the farm cats will be delighted to meet you. Anyway, I must be off now. Goodbye!'

Then, with a swish of his magnificent wings, he flew up into the night sky without a sound and floated silently out of sight.

Little One meets Henry and Harriet

NINE

Little One sat quietly on the branch for several minutes and thought about Oscar's warning. She seemed to remember that her mother had been very anxious about a fox when she was a tiny kitten on the farm in the country. She decided to take the wise old owl's advice and be extremely cautious; she had no wish to be caught by a sly old fox. Suddenly she heard a rustling sound coming from the ground below. Was that the fox already? She hoped he couldn't climb trees!

Peeping down through the leaves, she saw two small animals snuffling noisily about in the border near the garden wall. Little One was intrigued. The creatures appeared to be quite unaware of any danger, so she thought it was probably safe to investigate further. Feather-light, she sprang down from the branch onto the lawn below and silently made her way towards them.

They were strange-looking animals. Their bodies were covered with prickles and they had long pointed snouts and large bright black eyes. Just the other day, Mrs Gray's neighbour had described an animal like this. She had seen one in the garden the night before. She called it a hedgehog. Hedgehogs slept in their nest during the day and only came out at night to look for food, she said, and they were great to have in the garden because they ate creepy-crawlies like insects, slugs and worms and snails. UGH! They must be nocturnal creatures like Oscar, she decided.

Not wishing to alarm them, she called out softly. 'Hello there. Do you mind if I join you?'

'Please do,' one of them replied, 'but I shouldn't come too close, if I were you. I'm afraid we have fleas. They don't bother us because of our prickles, but if you caught them, they would drive you mad; you wouldn't be able to stop scratching.'

Little One stepped back hastily. She wanted to be friendly, but preferably at a safe distance. The thought of catching fleas did not appeal to her at all!

'I haven't seen you before. What are your names and where do you live?' she asked.

'I'm Henry and this is Harriet. We're very pleased to meet you,' Henry replied. 'We live here in the garden,' he went on. 'Our nest is tucked away out of sight behind the bushes. We sleep there during the day and come out at night to look for food for our babies and ourselves. During the winter, of course, you won't see us at all. That's when we hibernate.'

'What does that mean?' Little One asked.

'That's when we sleep in our nest all winter,' answered Harriet. 'We don't wake up until spring.'

'You must be starving when you wake up!' Little One said.

'You ask a lot of questions,' Henry remarked. 'Now it's our turn. Who are you and what are you doing here in our garden? We haven't seen you before.'

The cat introduced herself and told them about her adventure.

'That's very interesting,' said Harriet gravely, 'but I do hope you'll be sensible, dear. I'd be very worried if one of my children decided to go off on an adventure by themselves. Adventures may seem thrilling, but I'm sure they can be terrifying too. There are many dangers out here and you're not used to being out at night on your own. Everyone isn't as friendly as we are, you know. Suppose the fox appears out of nowhere! What would you do then?'

'Oscar warned me about him,' Little One replied. 'I intend to be extremely careful. I'll run like the wind and climb up the nearest tree in a flash, if he turns up. What does a fox look like? I've never seen one.'

'Oh, he's a handsome animal,' said Henry. 'There's no doubt about that. It's a pity he's so wicked. He looks as if butter wouldn't melt in his mouth. He has pointed ears and a sharp pointed nose. His coat is a beautiful reddish-brown colour with greyish-white underneath, and he has a lovely bushy tail with a white tip. Humans call it a brush because it's so thick. He seems ever so polite and friendly, but he'll pounce on you without warning in the twinkling of an eye! He's not to be trusted at all. Stay well away from him.'

'Don't worry; I intend to,' the cat answered. 'What would you do if you saw him?'

'Little One,' Henry continued, 'I've never met anyone who asks as many questions as you do! I sincerely hope you don't try to have a conversation with that fox. As a matter of fact, hedgehogs have poor eyesight. However, we have a good sense of smell and our hearing is excellent. We know when a fox is about because he has a very strong scent. When we sense danger we are able to roll ourselves into a prickly ball and that usually protects us from our enemies. We have to watch out for badgers, foxes and magpies, as well as tawny owls, as a matter of fact.'

Little One was surprised to hear that. She thought Oscar was such a nice old bird.

'Henry, dear,' Harriet interrupted, 'time's getting on and we have the little ones to feed. Would you like to try some of these worms and slugs, Little One? They're delicious.'

Little One shuddered at the thought of eating slimy black slugs and wriggly red worms. She much preferred the delicious salmon and prawns in jelly served by Mrs Gray in her shiny stainless-steel dish. Mrs Gray knew at once that she was hungry if she sat beside her dish looking hopeful. Sometimes she had to attract the old lady's attention by pushing her dish across the kitchen floor with her nose, but that was much easier than having to dig about in squelchy soil looking for something to eat. She thanked them politely for their kind invitation but said that she must be going.

'I intend to explore the windmill,' she announced. 'I've always wanted to see what's at the other side of the garden wall.'

'You'll be able to chat to the rabbits then,' Henry replied as he picked up a wriggling worm. 'They're very friendly little animals and they'll enjoy answering all your questions. Goodbye. We look forward to seeing you again before we settle down for our winter sleep.'

Their visitor averted her eyes as he popped the worm into his mouth and carried on digging in the border, munching away happily.

Little One meets Sam

TEN

Leaving Henry to enjoy his snack, Little One leaped up to the top of the garden wall and looked across at the hillside. In the moonlight the windmill seemed like a towering giant keeping watch over his kingdom. On the grass below there were so many rabbits that she lost count. She thought they were really delightful with their large bright eyes, their long floppy ears and their little twitching noses. She watched in silence for a while as they hopped about, their fluffy tails bobbing up and down as they went. Some of them were chasing each other, some were having fun fights and others were sitting quite still, quietly nibbling the grass. Henry had said that they would be friendly, so she made up her mind to join them. Without stopping to think, she jumped down and landed without a sound onto the grass below.

'Hey, watch where you're going! You nearly landed on my head!' a voice shouted from the shadows.

'I did no such thing,' Little One replied confidently.

'I've been practising for weeks and my landings are perfect. You're telling fibs.'

A little brown rabbit hopped out from the darkness and sat in front of her, twitching his nose and watching her intently with his large bright eyes.

'I know,' he replied, lowering his head in embarrassment. 'I'm sorry. I'm always getting into trouble for exaggerating. My mother says my tongue runs away with me. Actually, your landing was amazing. I've never seen you on our hill before. What's your name and why are you out at this time of night without your mother?'

Little One told him all about herself. She described her meetings with Oscar and Henry and Harriet and explained about her adventure.

'That's fantastic!' cried the little rabbit. 'You're really brave to go off by yourself, I must say. My mother, a female rabbit called a doe, thinks it's better to stay with your family. She says there's safety in numbers. In her opinion adventures might be fun, but they can also be frightening. I wish she'd let me have an adventure.' As he was speaking, a large grey rabbit hopped towards them.

'Sam,' the rabbit said in a cross voice, 'I'm tired of telling you not to wander away. Who is this? How many times do I have to tell you not to speak to strangers?'

'I'm sorry, Mother,' Sam replied meekly. 'This is my new friend, Little One. She's out on an adventure. Isn't it exciting?'

'You know what I think about adventures. You're not going on one and that's final!' his mother answered. 'Now remember what I said about wandering too far. If the fox comes, you know what to do. Listen for the signal. Don't forget.' After that she hopped away to join Sam's brothers and sisters, who were playing close by.

Little One was curious. 'What does your mother mean about the signal?' she asked.

'All rabbits are taught about the signal when they're tiny babies,' Sam said. 'It's very important, because it warns us when there is danger. If you look carefully you'll see an old buck, that's a male rabbit, standing up on the hilltop beside the windmill. He's on guard duty. As soon as he senses danger, he stamps on the ground with his back legs. When we hear the sound, we know that we have to run as fast as we can to our homes. There's another thing – if you look at my tail you'll notice that the fur underneath is white. When we're running away, the other rabbits see the white tails and they know that's a danger signal too.'

'I can't imagine why anyone should want to harm you,' Little One said.

'Don't you believe it! Rabbits make a very tasty meal,' answered Sam. 'We have lots of enemies. We have to watch out for humans, dogs, foxes and birds of prey like the eagle that can swoop down and grab us with their long talons in a flash! The eagle is a powerful bird with fantastic eyesight. He flies about looking for animals to feed himself and his family. He is particularly fond of baby rabbits. When he sees his prey, he swoops down and snatches up his victim with his sharp claws and flies off to his nest and his family. It's absolutely terrifying, there's no escape! And our enemies include tawny owls, I might add. Have you never heard that shocking nursery rhyme – "Bye Baby Bunting" – gone to get a rabbit skin, to wrap my little baby in? It's disgusting,' Sam said. 'My father said it's a crime!'

Little One was taken aback and very sad when she heard this. She had never thought that life in the outside world could be so difficult and cruel. Life with Mrs Gray might be boring, but at least it was safe. She did not have to eat grass or slugs and worms, dig in the soil for her food, or go out hunting for her meals – they were served on the dot!

'Where do you live?' she asked Sam. 'Do you have a nest like the hedgehogs?'

'No, silly.' Sam shook his head. 'Only the babies, which are called leverets, have nests. The rest of us live in a warren under the ground. Inside the hill there are lots of burrows all linking up with each other – amazing, isn't it? It's a bit confusing at first until you get used to it. My little sister's always getting lost. The females, that are called "does", make their nests at the end of a short burrow – "stops", they're called.'

'How do they make their nests?' Little One asked.

'My mother says I ask a lot of questions, but I think you're worse than me!' Sam told her. 'They make them with dried grass and tufts of their own fur,' he went on.

'They cover the opening with earth to keep their little ones safe while they're away. The trouble is that foxes know that there are babies inside and they dig them out sometimes.'

'That's terrible!' Little One cried. 'Foxes are cruel, aren't they?'

'You're right.' Sam nodded his head in agreement. 'That's why my mother is always checking up on me. Anyway, there aren't any foxes about at the moment. Let's go and play up beside the windmill. See if you can run as fast as me.'

Little One encounters the sly fox

ELEVEN

They played out in the moonlight for quite a long time. They chased each other round and round the windmill until they were out of breath, then they played hide and seek until at last Little One was so tired she said she must have a rest. She curled up and had a little catnap while Sam quietly nibbled the grass nearby. Little One was very happy. She was so pleased that she had made new friends. Her midnight adventure had been brilliant!

Suddenly she was startled by a loud thumping sound which echoed all around the hillside. It was the warning signal. The old buck on guard had sighted a fox prowling in the shadows at the bottom of the hill. Immediately the rabbits stopped what they were doing. For a split second they sat perfectly still, their noses twitching, their ears upright and then, in a flash of white tails, they disappeared into their burrows.

The frightened cat looked round desperately for a tree to climb, but the nearest tree was too far away in the next field. She knew that she would not be able to run as fast as the fox, who was racing up the hill like the wind in her direction. She was petrified. There was no escape! She remembered what Mrs Gray had said about her being snatched from the jaws of death when she was a kitten on the farm – it looked as if she was not going to be so lucky this time. Shaking with fear, she was unable to move from the spot as the fox came nearer and nearer…

Just then she heard a shout. It was Sam. His head was peeping out from a little hole in the ground. 'Run over here, quick!' he gasped.

In a panic she stumbled to the tiny opening and managed to squeeze herself in. Panting and quivering with fright, she crouched down beside him.

'This is an old stop,' Sam whispered. 'We'll have to stay here, I'm afraid. I can't take you into the warren, I'm sorry. It's against the rules. The elders won't allow it.'

Little One nodded her head. She was so breathless, she was unable to speak. At that precise moment she became aware of a strange scent, and looking up she saw two big gleaming eyes peering at her menacingly through the opening. The fox had discovered their hiding place! She thought of what Sam had said about foxes digging out baby rabbits from their nests. She wondered if this was the fox's plan. To her surprise the fox began to speak in a smooth, velvety voice. She observed his sharp, white teeth as he opened his exceedingly large mouth.

'Don't be frightened, my dears. I only want to be

your friend. It's such a beautiful night. Why don't you come out to play with me in the moonlight? It will be fun.'

The friends were trapped. There was no way out. What were they to do?

Suddenly they heard the deep, noisy barking of dogs nearby. They seemed to be coming closer and closer. To their relief, the fox stopped in his tracks. He lifted his head and sniffed the air with his long pointed nose, and then he shot up the hill in a flash and seemed to melt away into the shadows.

'Phew, that was scary!' Sam murmured with a sigh of relief. 'I must go now. My mother will be anxious about me. She'll be wondering where I am. I'll be in awful trouble when she sees me, but I expect she'll be very relieved. Goodbye. I hope I'll see you again soon.' Then he hopped away down into the burrow and was gone.

Little One meets the owlets

TWELVE

Little One sat very still for some time until she began to feel calm again. After a while, she squeezed through the entrance to the stop and set off down the hill towards the coast road. She was so near to the farm, she thought it would be nice to have a chat with the farm cats before she went back home. On the other hand, she might decide to stay with them. After all, she had come from a farm in the first place!

She jumped over the wall and landed on the pavement. Making sure that it was safe to cross the road, she bounded over and crawled under the gate into the farmer's field. There was the clump of trees where Oscar lived. The farm must be nearby. She guessed that she would probably find the cats in the barn. As she passed the trees, she heard a familiar voice. Looking up she saw Oscar perched on a branch. Sitting in a row on a branch below were three owlets.

'Hello there,' he called out. 'We're having flying and landing lessons. These three young ones need a lot of practice, I'm afraid. But come to think of it, I suppose I was just as awkward as they are, when I was their age.'

Little One nodded her head in agreement. She was certain that eventually they would be able to fly and land as beautifully as their parents. She watched them for a little while and was amused by their efforts. The owlets took a deep breath, closed their eyes and tumbled from the branch, flapping their wings furiously. Then they flopped to the ground in a heap. The three of them ended up rolling around with their legs waving about in the air, and they were giggling so much they could hardly stand up.

Now it was time to look for the farm cats! Little One said her goodbyes to the owl family and made her way to the farmyard. She slipped silently past the kennel where the old sheepdog lay snoozing peacefully, dreaming of the days when he was young and fit and able to hunt for rats and mice. She heard the horses snorting and stamping as she passed the stables. At last she reached the barn and went in. By the light of the moon shining through a little window, she saw three cats sitting on a bale of hay. The largest of them was an attractive marmalade cat with a snowy white chest and white paws. She looked as if she was wearing little white socks. The smallest cat had shiny black fur with a tiny spot of white on her forehead. The third one was a pretty tortoiseshell cat with a beautiful bushy tail. As Little One approached, the marmalade cat turned to speak to her.

'Hello there,' she said. 'What are you doing here? We don't often have visitors.' The visitor told her tale about being a farm cat herself, and how she wondered if she might stay with them. Then she told them about her adventure and her new friends.

'We'll discuss that later,' answered the marmalade cat. 'First of all we'd better introduce ourselves. Our little friend here is called Eclipse because she's so dark. She's rather shy and doesn't say very much.'

'My name is Olivia,' said the tortoiseshell cat in a ladylike voice. 'I'm very pleased to meet you.'

'I'm Gypsy,' the marmalade cat continued. 'I've lived on the farm for years, so I'm well past my sell-by date, as you can imagine. In my younger days I used to go across to the windmill to search for rats, but I'm too old for all that now. The others are much younger than me, so I leave all the hunting to them.' Just then another cat limped into the barn.

'Oh, here's Cuddles,' she remarked. 'Have you ever seen a cat like him before?'

Little One had to admit that she had not. He certainly did not look like a cuddly cat to her. He had a torn ear and one of his legs had obviously been injured at some time. He had dirty white fur with patches of grey and to her mind he looked absolutely disgusting. But naturally she was too polite to say so.

'Cuddles was the pet kitten in the farmhouse at one time,' Gypsy went on. 'The children gave him his name because he was so sweet and fluffy and cuddly.

Unfortunately when he began to go out into the farmyard, he liked sitting under the cars and tractors and got absolutely filthy. He couldn't be bothered to wash himself, so Mrs Williams the farmer's wife refused to have him in the house and he's lived here with us ever since.' Olivia interrupted at this point.

'One should never judge by appearances,' she said, having noted the expression on their visitor's face. 'He's lovely, really. He's so kind and thoughtful. If we're too tired to go out looking for mice, he brings them back for us. There aren't many cats that would do that.'

Little One was ashamed of her rudeness. She would be more careful about making instant judgements in future.

'Now what's all this about adventures?' Gypsy remarked. 'Adventures may sound wonderful at your age, but if you ask me, your experience with the fox sounds horrifying. You've had a very lucky escape, in my opinion. You were rather foolish to go off on your own like that; and as for wanting to stay on the farm with us, you should think again.'

At that moment Eclipse began to speak, to everyone's astonishment.

'I can't understand why anyone should want to live in a draughty old barn like this, when they can stay in a warm, comfortable home with a kind human to love them and care for them. It's not too bad in the summer, but in the winter this place is absolutely freezing. I wouldn't mind changing places with you.'

Then Olivia joined in. 'And what about meals?' she asked. 'I expect your meals are served whenever Mrs Gray thinks you're hungry. We don't know where our next meal is coming from. We even have to rummage around in the dustbins for something to eat sometimes and it's no fun chasing about trying to catch mice and rats when you're starving and feeling worn out. I can tell you.'

Just then there was a loud rumbling sound. 'I thought there was a storm brewing,' Cuddles murmured. 'I could feel it in my bones.' Little One was scared. She was beginning to wish that she was back at home safe and sound with Mrs Gray.

Suddenly there was a terrific flash of lightning which lit up the gloomy barn, and then there was a deafening crack of thunder above their heads. It was so loud that Little One was convinced that the roof was about to collapse on top of them. The lightning flashed again, followed by another tremendous crash of thunder.

As she shook with terror, Cuddles said to her kindly, 'Don't be frightened. The children used to tell me that it's only the clouds bumping into each other.'

'My granny told me that it was the angels moving the furniture about in Heaven,' Eclipse joined in.

Gypsy knew that they were just stories, but as their visitor was so terrified, she thought it best to leave the correct explanation for another time.

Then the rain began to pour down in torrents, drumming noisily on the barn roof, splashing against the window and gurgling down the drainpipes. The barn felt cold and damp and Little One began to shiver. She was beginning to feel thoroughly miserable and she wished that she was back in the tiny flat curled up in her soft, cosy pink chair. Cuddles tried to cheer her up by bringing her a little mouse to eat. She was touched by his kindness but refused courteously.

'Thank you,' she said. 'It's very sweet of you, but I'm not terribly hungry at the moment.' She could not have eaten the little mouse, even if she had been given a thousand pounds, but she thought it would be rude to tell him so.

'You'd better stay here with us until morning,' Gypsy suggested. 'You might as well wait until the rain stops. It's much too early to go back home now anyway. Mrs Gray will still be in bed and you'll just have to sit outside until she gets up.'

At last the rain did stop and all the cats curled up on the bale of hay and nodded off to sleep. When Little One opened her eyes, the sunlight was shining through the little window and she could hear the birds stirring in the trees nearby.

Gypsy sat beside her and whispered softly, 'You'd better be going now, while it's safe to cross the road. There'll be a lot of traffic later on and we don't want you to have an accident, do we? Goodbye, my dear. I hope we'll meet again sometime.'

Little One encounters the magpie on her way home

THIRTEEN

Little One thanked all the cats for their kindness and then she set off on her journey home. She hurried through the farmyard, past the stables and the snoozing sheepdog, past the trees where Oscar and his family were tucked up asleep, until she arrived at the coast road. Gypsy was right; the road was quiet at this time of the morning. She flew across and at last she reached the hill. All the rabbits had vanished and the deserted windmill stood silently gazing out to sea.

A glorious crimson sun was rising up from the horizon, throwing a kaleidoscope of reflected colours across the sky. Everything was calm and peaceful. Only a solitary seagull wheeled noiselessly above in the early morning air. Little One stopped for a moment and thought how beautiful the world was and how lucky she was to be going back home. Leaping over the garden wall, she was just in time to catch a glimpse of Henry and Harriet as they scuttled back to their nest behind the bushes.

She raced across the lawn and spotted the familiar long tail and dazzling white chest of the dreaded magpie perched high on the rooftop inspecting his territory. Luckily, she ran like the wind and she was so fast that he failed to notice her. At last she arrived in the front garden and crept under the hydrangea bush, from which she had a clear view of Mrs Gray's front door. She waited patiently until Mrs Gray came downstairs to collect her milk.

After a while the door opened and Mrs Gray appeared. Little One was delighted to see her and rushed across the grass to greet her, mewing loudly with relief. Little One would have loved to have been able to tell Mrs Gray about her adventure, but it was impossible. Animals are able to talk to each other in stories, but not to people.

Of course, the old lady was overjoyed to see her pet. She scooped her up in her arms and gave her a very welcome cuddle. As soon as they went upstairs Little One was given a bowl of milk and a dish of her favourite salmon and prawns. Then they both sat in the pink velvet chair. The runaway cat settled down on Mrs Gray's knee and snuggled under her chin, looking up at her with her great green eyes and purring with happiness.

She had decided the best way to see the outside world was from the security of the kitchen windowsill – until next time, perhaps!

ABOUT THE AUTHOR

Edna Dent was born in Sunderland on 23 July 1935. She grew up and went to school locally and went on to become a teacher, teaching both in her hometown and Leeds, where she lived for a while. Edna retired from teaching due to failing eyesight and enjoyed her social life with a small group of cherished friends.

She was keen to write a story that would enthral children and educate them at the same time. *Little One, A Cat's Tale* is based on a real-life cat that lived with Edna during the 1990s. Although Edna had owned cats all her life, this one was particularly interesting. It was indeed abandoned as a farm cat and was initially called 'Little One' due to its small frame but was later named Mitzi by Edna's daughter Lydia. She was very affectionate (some cats are not so) and she would always stand at the top of the stairs to greet Edna when she returned home. Importantly, she filled a gap in Edna's life at a time when she needed it most.

Many of the adventures described within Mrs Gray's flat did take place, although what happened on Little

One's adventures outside is something born out of the author's imagination. She wrote this story in 2010 and it sat on an electronic shelf for ten years. After a lot of encouragement from one friend in particular, Rhoda Bowman, she dusted down the manuscript and decided to get it published. With the help and support of her nephew Andrew, she has finally seen her dream come true.

Edna hopes this little book will help young children learn about the importance of love and friendship and go a little way to helping them see that adventures can be both fun and a bit scary at times. Ultimately her wish is to bring some joy and smiles to faces of children and adults alike.

ACKNOWLEDGEMENTS

Clive Rand:
For his incredible illustrations and artistry in bringing to life all the wonderful creatures Little One meets on her adventure. His generous time and dedication has been truly appreciated. His kindness for merely asking for a donation to the RNLI for his creative work is warmly welcomed and appreciated for a cause very close to my heart.

Rhoda Bowman:
Without my dear friend's encouragement, this book would never have been completed.

Andrew Akal:
Without my nephew's help and support, this book would not have been published. Thank you for your love and care when all seemed lost.